The name Star Bright Books and the Star Bright Books logo
are registered trademarks of Star Bright Books, Inc.
Please visit: www.starbrightbooks.com.
For bulk orders, please email: orders@starbrightbooks.com,
or call customer service at: (617) 354-1300.

Printed on paper from sustainable forests.

Hardback ISBN-13: 978-1-59572-789-3
Paperback ISBN-13: 978-1-59572-790-9
Star Bright Books / MA / 00111170
Printed in China / WKT / 9 8 7 6 5 4 3 2 1

Library of Congress Cataloging-in-Publication Data

Names: Tebbit, Jake, author, illustrator.
Title: Woolly the wide awake sheep / Jake Tebbit.
Description: Cambridge, Massachusetts : Star Bright Books, 2017. |
Summary:
 Wide awake yet again, Woolly the sheep asks his barnyard friends how
they lull themselves to sleep.
Identifiers: LCCN 2017047329| ISBN 9781595727893 (hardcover) | ISBN
 9781595727909 (pbk.)
Subjects: | CYAC: Bedtime--Fiction. | Sleep--Fiction. | Sheep--Fiction. |
 Domestic animals--Fiction.
Classification: LCC PZ8.3.T21843 Wo 2017 | DDC [E]--dc23
LC record available at https://lccn.loc.gov/2017047329

Woolly

THE
WIDE AWAKE SHEEP

JAKE TEBBIT

STAR BRIGHT BOOKS
CAMBRIDGE Massachusetts

This is the tale of Woolly the sheep,
who could never, ever just nod off to sleep.

Not ever? No, never!

Poor Woolly the sheep!

As the flock slept, away Woolly crept,
being careful to cause no alarm.

Not wanting to wait,

he jumped over the gate...

and ran all the way up

to the barn.

Bertie the bull, eating cake in his stall,
was surprised to see Woolly the sheep.

"Bertie," asked Woolly. "Don't think me silly,
but how do you get off to sleep?"

"Simple," said Bertie. "At around 6:30, if I'm
awake and can't fall asleep—I count sheep."

Said Connie with a moo,

"It's troooooo! It's troooooo!

Take the word of a cow, if you want to know how.

When I'm wide awake and can't fall asleep—

I count sheep!"

"I will ask Kitty,
the old farm cat,
who naps through the day
and will know what to say."

"Kitty, do tell,
how you sleep so well."

"It's just a cat's way,"
Kitty replied with a sigh.
"On the rare night I'm wide
awake and can't fall asleep—
I count sheep!"

Above Kitty the cat, Sally the spider sat.

She dropped down on her silken trapeze.

"Once I've woven my web,
 and I'm ready for bed,
I try counting all of my knees.
But if I'm wide awake and can't sleep
—I count sheep."

"Cluck, cluck!"

Hattie the hen flew into the pen.

"Woolly, my dear, I did overhear, so, I'll say it all over again. When I'm wide awake and can't fall asleep—I count sheep."

A sad Woolly trudged back to the meadow.

"What's up, my poor little fellow?" asked Granddaddy Ram.

"I'm tired," Woolly said with a sigh.

"I can't fall asleep!"

"I try and I try, and just don't know why.
So I asked all my friends on the farm.

I asked Bertie the bull and Connie the cow,   Kitty the cat,

Sally the spider,   and Hattie the hen . . .

and I got the same answer,
again and again.

When they're wide awake
and can't fall asleep—
they count sheep."

"Well, I have a plan," said Granddaddy Ram.
"Have you tried counting sheep, like they do?"

Woolly shook his sad head, "I don't think
that I can. I'm tired and I haven't a clue."

"But how will you know, if you don't have a go?
I think that you really should try."

"Together, shall we, from the shade of this tree,

count sheep as they pass by?"

"Now look...

a lamb with his mother... and there is his brother.

Do you agree—that makes three?

And there is one more—that makes four."

"Five and six by those sticks,

seven and eight by the gate,

nine and ten...but not Hattie the hen!

Don't count Hattie—she's not a sheep."

"Now, Woolly, it's your turn to count sheep." Then Granddaddy Ram looked down, only to see—

Woolly the sheep . . .

fast asleep!